The Cavalry General

Xenophon

Table of Contents

The Cavalry General

zen–e–fan

Xenophon

Kessinger Publishing reprints thousands of hard–to–find books!

Visit us at http://www.kessinger.net

Translation by H. G. Dakyns

Xenophon the Athenian was born 431 B.C. He was a pupil of Socrates. He marched with the Spartans, and was exiled from Athens. Sparta gave him land and property in Scillus, where he lived for many years before having to move once more, to settle in Corinth. He died in 354 B.C.

The Cavalry General is a discourse on the merits a cavalry general, or hipparch, in Athens should have. Xenophon also describes the development of a cavalry force, and some tactical details to be applied in the field and in festival exhibition.

THE DUTIES OF A HIPPARCH[1]

The Cavalry General

or

Commander of Cavalry at Athens

I

Your first duty is to offer sacrifice, petitioning the gods to grant you such good gifts[2] as shall enable you in thought, word, and deed to discharge your office in the manner most acceptable to Heaven, and with fullest increase to yourself, and friends, and to the state at large of affection, glory, and wide usefulness. The goodwill of Heaven[3] so obtained, you shall proceed to mount your troopers, taking care that the full complement which the law demands is reached, and that the normal force of cavalry is not diminished. There will need to be a reserve of remounts, or else a deficiency may occur at any moment,[4] looking to the fact that some will certainly succumb to old age, and others, from one reason or another, prove unserviceable.

[1] For the title, etc., see Schneid. "Praemon. de Xeno." {Ipp}.
   Boeckh, "P. E. A." 251.

[2] Or, "with sacrifice to ask of Heaven those gifts of thought and
   speech and conduct whereby you will exercise your office most
   acceptably to the gods themselves, and with . . ." Cf. Plat.
   "Phaedr." 273 E; "Euthr." 14 B.

[3] The Greek phrase is warmer, {theon d' ileon onton}, "the gods
   being kindly and propitious." Cf. Plat. "Laws," 712 B.

[4] Lit. "at any moment there will be too few." See "Les Cavaliers
   Atheniens," par Albert Martin, p. 308.

But now suppose the complement of cavalry is levied,[5] the duty will devolve on you of seeing, in the first place, that your horses are well fed and in condition to stand their work, since a horse which cannot endure fatigue will clearly be unable to overhaul the foeman or effect escape;[6] and in the second place, you will have to see to it the animals are tractable, since, clearly again, a horse that will not obey is only fighting for the enemy and not his friends. So, again, an animal that kicks when mounted must be cast; since brutes of that sort may often do more mischief than the foe himself. Lastly, you must pay attention to the horses' feet, and see that they will stand being ridden over rough ground. A horse, one knows, is practically useless where he cannot be galloped without suffering.

[5] Lit. "in process of being raised."

[6] Or, "to press home a charge a l'outrance, or retire from the field
    unscathed."

And now, supposing that your horses are all that they ought to be, like pains must be applied to train the men themselves. The trooper, in the first place, must be able to spring on horseback easily—a feat to which many a man has owed his life ere now. And next, he must be able to ride with freedom over every sort of ground, since any description of country may become the seat of war. When, presently, your men have got firm seats, your aim should be to make as many members of the corps as possible not only skilled to hurl the javelin from horseback with precision, but to perform all other feats expected of the expert horseman. Next comes the need to arm both horse and man in such a manner as to minimise the risk of wounds, and yet to increase the force of every blow delivered.[7] This attended to, you must contrive to make your men amenable to discipline, without which neither good horses, nor a firm seat, nor splendour of equipment will be of any use at all.

[7] Lit. "so that whilst least likely to be wounded themselves, they
    may most be able to injure the enemy."

The general of cavalry,[8] as patron of the whole department, is naturally responsible for its efficient working. In view, however, of the task imposed upon that officer had he to carry out these various details single–handed, the state has chosen to associate[9] with him certain coadjutors in the persons of the phylarchs (or tribal captains),[10] and has besides imposed upon the senate a share in the superintendence of the cavalry. This being so, two things appear to me desirable; the first is, so to work upon the phylarch that he shall share your own enthusiasm for the honour of the corps;[11] and secondly, to have at your disposal in the senate able orators,[12] whose language may instil a wholesome fear into the knights themselves, and thereby make them all the better men, or tend to pacify the senate on occasion and disarm unseasonable anger.

[8] See "Mem." III. iii.

[9] Cf. Theophr. xxix. "The Oligarchic Man": "When the people are deliberating whom they shall associate with the archon as joint directors of the procession." (Jebb.)

[10] Or, "squadron—leaders."

[11] "Honour and prestige of knighthood."

[12] "To keep a staff of orators." Cf. "Anab." VII. vi. 41; "Cyrop." I. vi. 19; "Hell." VI. ii. 39.

The above may serve as memoranda[13] of the duties which will claim your chief attention. How the details in each case may best be carried out is a further matter, which I will now endeavour to explain.

[13] "A sort of notes and suggestions," "mementoes." Cf. "Horsemanship," iii. 1, xii. 14.

As to the men themselves—the class from which you make your pick of troopers—clearly according to the law you are bound to enrol "the ablest" you can find "in point of wealth and bodily physique"; and "if not by persuasion, then by prosecution in a court of law."[14] And for my part, I think, if legal pressure is to be applied, you should apply it in those cases where neglect to prosecute might fairly be ascribed to interested motives;[15] since if you fail to put compulsion on the greater people first, you leave a backdoor of escape at once to those of humbler means. But there will be other cases;[16] say, of young men in whom a real enthusiasm for the service may be kindled by recounting to them all the brilliant feats of knighthood; while you may disarm the opposition of their guardians by dwelling on the fact that, if not you, at any rate some future hipparch will certainly compel them to breed horses,[17] owing to their wealth; whereas, if they enter the service[18] during your term of office, you will undertake to deter their lads from mad extravagance in buying horses,[19] and take pains to make good horsemen of them without loss of time; and while pleading in this strain, you must endeavour to make your practice correspond with what you preach.

[14] Lit. "by bringing them into court, or by persuasion," i.e. by
legal if not by moral pressure. See Martin, op. cit. pp. 316, 321
foll.

[15] i.e. "would cause you to be suspected of acting from motives of
gain."

[16] Reading {esti de kai ous}, or if as vulg. {eti de kai}, "More
than that, it strikes me one may work on the feelings of young
fellows in such a way as to disarm." See Hartmann, "An. Xen. N."
325.

[17] Cf. Aesch. "P. V." 474; Herod. vi. 35; Dem. 1046. 14; Thuc. vi.
12; Isocr. {peri tou zeugous}, 353 C. {ippotrophein d'
epikheiresas, o ton eudaimonestaton ergon esti.} See Prof. Jebb's
note to Theophr. "Ch." vi. p. 197, note 16.

[18] Lit. "if they mount."

[19] Like that of Pheidippides in the play; see Aristoph. "Clouds," 23
foll. And for the price of horses, ranging from 3 minas (= L12
circa) for a common horse, or 12 minas (say L50) for a good saddle
or race–horse, up to the extravagant sum of 13 talents (say 3000
guineas) given for "Bucephalus," see Boeckh, "P. E. A." (Eng. tr.)
p. 74. Cf. Isaeus, 55. 22; 88. 17; Lys. "de Maled." 133. 10; Aul.
Gell. "Noct. Att." v. 2.

To come to the existing body of knights,[20] it would tend,[21] I think, to better rearing
and more careful treatment of their horses if the senate issued a formal notice that for the
future twice the amount of drill will be required, and that any horse unable to keep up
will be rejected. And so, too, with regard to vicious horses, I should like to see an edict
promulgated to the effect that all such animals will be rejected. This threat would
stimulate the owners of such brutes to part with them by sale, and, what is more, to
exercise discretion at the time of purchase. So, too, it would be a good thing if the same

threat of rejection were made to include horses that kick on the exercising–grounds, since it is impossible to keep such animals in the ranks; and in case of an advance against a hostile force at any point,[22] they must perforce trail in the rear, so that, thanks to the vice of the animal which he bestrides, the trooper himself is rendered useless.

[20] Or, "As regards those who are actually serving in the cavalry."
    For a plausible emend. of this passage (S. 13) see Courier ("Notes
    sur le texte," p. 54); L. Dind. ad loc.

[21] Lit. "the senate might incite to . . ."

[22] Reading {ean}, or if {kan} with the MSS., trans. "even in case of
    an advance against the enemy."

With a view to strengthening the horses' feet: if any one has an easier or more simple treatment to suggest, by all means let it be adopted; but for myself, as the result of experience, I maintain that the proper course is to lay down a loose layer of cobbles from the road, a pound or so in weight, on which the horse should be put to stand, when taken from the manger to be groomed.[23] The point is, that the horse will keep perpetually moving first one foot and then another on the stones, whilst being rubbed down or simply because he is fidgeted by flies. Let any one try the experiment, and, I venture to predict, not only will he come to trust my guidance, but he will see his horse's hoofs grow just as round and solid as the cobbles.

[23] See below, "Horse." iv. 4. The Greeks did not "shoe" their
    horses.

Assuming, then, your horses are all that horses ought to be, how is the trooper to attain a like degree of excellence? To that question I will now address myself. The art of leaping on to horseback is one which we would fain persuade the youthful members of the corps to learn themselves; though, if you choose to give them an instructor,[24] all the greater credit to yourself. And as to the older men you cannot do better than accustom them to mount, or rather to be hoisted up by aid of some one, Persian fashion.[25]

[24] Like Pheidon, in the fragment of Mnesimachus's play "The Breeder
    of Horses," ap. Athen. See Courier, ib. p. 55.

[25] See "Anab." IV. iv. 4; "Horsemanship," vi. 12.

With a view to keeping a firm seat on every sort of ground, it may be perhaps be thought a little irksome to be perpetually marching out, when there is no war;[26] but all the same, I would have you call your men together and impress upon them the need to train themselves, when they ride into the country to their farms, or elsewhere, by leaving the high road and galloping at a round pace on ground of every description.[27] This method will be quite as beneficial to them as the regular march out, and at the same time not produce the same sense of tedium. You may find it useful also to remind them that the state on her side is quite willing to expend a sum of nearly forty talents[28] yearly, so that in the event of war she may not have to look about for cavalry, but have a thoroughly efficient force to hand for active service. Let these ideas be once instilled into their minds, and, mark my words, your trooper will fall with zest to practising horsemanship, so that if ever the flame of war burst out he may not be forced to enter the lists a raw recruit, unskilled to fight for fame and fatherland or even life itself.

[26] In the piping days of peace.

[27] See "Econ." xi. 17. Cf. Theophr. "Ch." viii. "The Late Learner":
{kai eis agron eph' ippou allotriou katakhoumenos ama meletan
ippazesthai, kai peson ten kephalon kateagenai}, "Riding into the
country on another's horse, he will practise his horsemanship by
the way, and falling, will break his head" (Jebb).

[28] = L10,000 circa. See Boeckh, op. cit. p. 251.

It would be no bad thing either, to forewarn your troopers that one day you will take them out yourself for a long march, and lead them across country over every kind of ground. Again, whilst practising the evolutions of the rival cavalry display,[29] it will be well to gallop out at one time to one district and again to another. Both men and horses will be benefited.

[29] Lit. "the anthippasia." See iii. 11, and "Horsemanship," viii.
10.

Next, as to hurling the javelin from horseback, the best way to secure as wide a practice of the art as possible, it strikes me, would be to issue an order to your phylarchs that it will be their duty to put themselves at the head of the marksmen of several tribes, and to ride out to the butts for practice. In this way a spirit of emulation will be roused—the several officers will, no doubt, be eager to turn out as many marksmen as they can to aid the state.[30]

[30] On competition cf. "Cyrop." II. i. 22, and our author passim.

And so too, to ensure that splendour of accoutrement which the force requires,[31] the greatest help may once again be looked for from the phylarchs; let these officers but be persuaded that from the public point of view the splendid appearance of their squadrons[32] will confer a title to distinction far higher than that of any personal equipment. Nor is it reasonable to suppose that they will be deaf to such an argument, since the very desire to hold the office of phylarch itself proclaims a soul alive to honour and ambition. And what is more, they have it in their power, in accordance with the actual provisions of the law, to equip their men without the outlay of a single penny, by enforcing that self–equipment out of pay[33] which the law prescribes.

[31] Or, "a beauty of equipment, worthy of our knights." Cf. Aristoph.
    "Lysistr." 561, and a fragment of "The Knights," of Antiphanes,
    ap. Athen. 503 B, {pant' 'Amaltheias keras}. See "Hiero," ix. 6;
    "Horse." xi. 10.

[32] Lit. "tribes," {phulai} (each of the ten tribes contributing
    about eighty men, or, as we might say, a squadron).

[33] i.e. the {katastasis}, "allowance," so technically called. Cf.
    Lys. "for Mantitheos"; Jebb, "Att. Or." i. 246; Boeckh, "P. E. A."
    II. xxi. p. 263; K. F. Hermann, 152, 19; Martin, op. cit. p. 341.

But to proceed. In order to create a spirit of obedience in your subordinates, you have two formidable instruments;[34] as a matter of plain reason you can show them what a host of blessings the word discipline implies; and as a matter of hard fact you can, within the limits of the law, enable the well–disciplined to reap advantage, while the undisciplined are made to feel the pinch at every turn.

[34] "The one theoretic, the other practical."

But if you would rouse the emulation of your phylarchs, if you would stir in each a personal ambition to appear at the head of his own squadron in all ways splendidly appointed, the best incentive will be your personal example. You must see to it that your own bodyguard[35] are decked with choice accoutrement and arms; you must enforce on them the need to practise shooting pertinaciously; you must expound to them the theory of the javelin, yourself an adept in the art through constant training.[36]

[35] Techn. {prodromoi}, possibly = the Hippotoxotai, or corps of 200
    mounted archers—Scythians; cf. "Mem." III. iii. 11. Or, probably,
    "mounted skirmishers," distinct from the {ippotexotai}. Cf.
    Arrian, "An." i. 12. 7. See Aristot. "Ath. Pol." 49. 5.

[36] Reading as vulg. {eisegoio}, or if with L. D. {egoio} (cf. above,
    S. 21), trans. "you must lead them out to the butts yourself."

Lastly, were it possible to institute and offer prizes to the several tribal squadrons in reward for every excellence of knighthood known to custom in the public spectacles of our city, we have here, I think, an incentive which will appeal to the ambition of every true Athenian. How small, in the like case of our choruses, the prizes offered, and yet how great the labour and how vast the sums expended![37] But we must discover umpires of such high order that to win their verdict will be as precious to the victor as victory itself.

[37] See "Hell." III. iv. 15; "Hiero," ix. 3; "Cyrop." I. vi. 18;
    Martin, op. cit. p. 260 f.

II

Given, then, that your troopers are thoroughly trained in all the above particulars, it is necessary, I presume, that they should further be instructed in a type of evolution the effect of which will show itself not only in the splendour of the great processions[1] in honour of the gods, but in the manouvres of the exercising–ground; in the valorous onslaught of real battle when occasion calls; and in the ease with which whole regiments will prosecute their march, or cross a river, or thread a defile without the slightest symptom of confusion. What this formation is—essential, at least in my opinion, to the noblest execution of their several duties—I will now, without delay, endeavour to explain.[2]

[1] e.g. the Panathenaic, as depicted on the frieze of the Parthenon.

[2] Or, "what this best order is, the adoption of which will give
these several features fair accomplishment, I will without further
pause set forth."

We take as our basis, then, the constitutional division of ten tribes.[3] Given these, the proper course, I say, is to appoint, with the concurrence of the several phylarchs, certain decadarchs (file–leaders)[4] to be selected from the men ripest of age and strength, most eager to achieve some deed of honour and to be known to fame. These are to form your front–rank men;[5] and after these, a corresponding number should be chosen from the oldest and the most sagacious members of the squadron, to form the rear–rank of the files or decads; since, to use an illustration, iron best severs iron when the forefront of the blade[6] is strong and tempered, and the momentum at the back is sufficient.

[3] See "Revenues," iv. 30.

[4] Decadarchs, lit. commanders of ten, a "file" consisting normally
(or ideally) of ten men. Cf. "Cyrop. II. ii. 30; VIII. i. 14. It
will be borne in mind that a body of cavalry would, as a rule, be
drawn up in battle line at least four deep (see "Hell." III. iv.
13), and frequently much deeper. (The Persian cavalry in the
engagement just referred to were twelve deep.)

[5] See "Cyrop." III. iii. 41, 57; VI. iii. 24, 27; VII. i. 15; "Pol.
Lac." xi. 5. These front–rank men would seem to correspond to our
"troop guides," and the rear–rank men to our serre–files to some
extent.

[6] Cf. Aelian Tact. 26, ap. Courier.

The Cavalry General

The interval between the front and rear–rank men will best be filled supposing that the decadarchs are free to choose their own supports, and those chosen theirs, and so on following suit; since on this principle we may expect each man to have his trustiest comrade at his back.

As to your lieutenant,[7] it is every way important to appoint a good man to this post, whose bravery will tell; and in case of need at any time to charge the enemy, the cheering accents of his voice will infuse strength into those in front; or when the critical moment of retreat arrives, his sage conduct in retiring will go far, we may well conclude, towards saving his division.[8]

[7] {ton aphegoumenon}, lit. "him who leads back" (a function which
    would devolve upon the {ouragos} under many circumstances). Cf.
    "Cyrop." II. iii. 21; "Hell." IV. viii. 37; Plat. "Laws," 760 D. =
    our "officer serre–file," to some extent. So Courier: "Celui qui
    commande en serre–file. C'est chez nous le capitaine en second."

[8] Or, "the rest of the squadron." Lit. "his own tribesmen."

An even number of file–leaders will admit of a greater number of equal subdivisions than an odd.

The above formation pleases me for two good reasons: in the first place, all the front–rank men are forced to act as officers;[9] and the same man, mark you, when in command is somehow apt to feel that deeds of valour are incumbent on him which, as a private, he ignores; and in the next place, at a crisis when something calls for action on the instant, the word of command passed not to privates but to officers takes speedier effect.

[9] i.e. all find themselves in a position of command, and there is
    nothing like command to inspire that feeling of noblesse oblige
    which is often lacking in the private soldier. See Thuc. v. 66;
    "Pol. Lac." xi. 5.

Supposing, then, a regiment of cavalry drawn up in this formation: just as the squadron–leaders have their several positions for the march (or the attack[10]) assigned them by the commander, so the file– leaders will depend upon the captain for the order passed along the line in what formation they are severally to march; and all being prearranged by word of mouth, the whole will work more smoothly than if left to chance—like people crowding out of a theatre to their mutual annoyance. And when it comes to actual encounter greater promptitude will be displayed: supposing the attack is made in front, by the file–leaders who know that this is their appointed post; or in case of danger suddenly appearing in rear, then by the rear–rank men, whose main idea is that to desert one's post is base. A want of orderly arrangement, on the contrary, leads to confusion worse confounded at every narrow road, at every passage of a river; and when it comes to fighting, no one of his own free will assigns himself his proper post in face of an enemy.

[10] Lit. "where to ride," i.e. in what formation whether on the line
     of march or in action.

The above are fundamental matters not to be performed without the active help of every trooper who would wish to be a zealous and unhesitating fellow–worker with his officer.[11]

[11] Cf. "Hiero," vii. 2; "Cyrop." II. iv. 10.

III

I come at length to certain duties which devolve upon the general of cavalry himself in person: and first and foremost, it concerns him to obtain the favour of the gods by sacrifices in behalf of the state cavalry; and in the next place to make the great procession at the festivals a spectacle worth seeing; and further, with regard to all those public shows demanded by the state, wherever held,[1] whether in the grounds of the Acadamy or the Lyceum, at Phaleron or within the hippodrome, it is his business as commander of the knights to see that every pageant of the sort is splendidly exhibited.

[1] Cf. Theophr. "Ch." vii. (Jebb ad loc. p. 204, n. 25).

But these, again, are memoranda.[2] To the question how the several features of the pageant shall receive their due impress of beauty, I will now address myself.

[2] Read {tauta men alla upomnemata}, or if with Pantazid. {apla},
   trans. "these are simply memoranda."

And first to speak of the Processions.[3] These will, I think, be rendered most acceptable to Heaven and to earth's spectators were the riders to ride round the Agora and temples, commencing from the Hermae, and pay honour to the sacred beings, each in turn, whose shrines and statues are there congregated. (Thus in the great Dionysia[4] the choruses embrace their gracious service to the other gods and to the Twelve with circling dance.[5]) When the circuit is completed, and the riders are back again in front of the Hermae, it would add, I think, to the beauty of the scene[6] if at this point they formed in companies of tribes, and giving their horses rein, swept forward at the gallop to the Eleusinion. Nor must I omit to note the right position of the lance, to lessen as far as possible the risk of mutual interference.[7] Each trooper should hold his lance straight between the ears of his charger, which in proportion to the distinctness given to the weapon will rouse terror, and at the same time create a vague idea of multitudinousness.[8]

[3] {tas pompas}. See A. Martin, op. cit. 147, 160.

[4] Celebrated in March (Elaphebolion).

[5] Or, "by dancing roundelays in honour of the gods, especially The
   Twelve"; and as to the Twelve cf. Aristoph. "Knights," 235,
   "Birds," 95; Plat. "Laws," 654; Paus. i. 3. 3; 40. 3; viii. 25. 3;
   Plut. "Nic." 13; Lycurg. 198.

[6] Or, "it would be a beautiful sequel to the proceedings, in my
   opinion, if at this point they formed in squadron column, and
   giving rein to their chargers, swept forward at full gallop to the
   Eleusinion." See Leake, op. cit. i. 296.

[7] Lit. "nor will I omit how the lances shall as little as possible
   overlap one another."

[8] Lit. "Every trooper should be at pains to keep his lance straight
   between the ears of his charger, if these weapons are to be

distinct and terror–striking, and at the same time to appear numerous."

As soon as they have ceased from the charge at full gallop, the pace should at once be changed; and now, with footing slow, let them retrace their course back to the temples. In this way every detail characteristic of knightly pageantry[9] will have been displayed to the delight of god and man. That our knights are not accustomed to these actual evolutions, I am well aware; but I also recognise the fact that the performances are good and beautiful and will give pleasure to spectators. I do not fail to note, moreover, that novel feats of horsemanship have before now been performed by our knights, when their commanders have had the ability to get their wishes readily complied with.

[9] Lit. "everything that may be performed on a mounted horse."
  Possibly, as Cobet suggests, {kala} has dropped out. See
  "Horsemanship," xi. 3, 6.

But now, let us suppose it is the occasion of the march–past,[10] in the grounds of the Lyceum, before the javelin–throwing. The scene would gain in beauty if the tribal squadrons were to ride in line of columns[11] as if for battle, in two divisions, five squadrons in the one and five in the other, with the hipparch and the phylarchs at their head, in such formation as to allow the whole breadth of the racecourse to be filled. Then, as soon as they have gained the top[12] of the incline, which leads down to the theatre opposite, it would, I think, be obviously useful here to show the skill with which your troopers can gallop down a steep incline[13] with as broad a front as the nature of the ground permits. I am quite clear that your troopers, if they can trust their own skill in galloping, will take kindly to such an exhibition; while as certainly, if unpractised, they must look to it that the enemy does not give them a lesson in the art some day, perforce.

[10] {dielaunosin en Lukeio}. See A. Martin, op. cit. 196; cf. Arist.
  "Peace," 356.

[11] Or, as we might say, "in regimental order," "with the commanding
  officer in front and their respective squadron–leaders"; and for
  the Lyceum see "Hell." I. i. 33; II. iv. 27.

[12] Lit. "the apex of the confronting theatre."

14

[13] See "Horsemanship," viii. 6; "Anab." IV. viii. 28.

To come to the test manouvres.[14] The order in which the men will ride with showiest effect on these occasions has been already noted.[15] As far as the leader is himself concerned, and presuming he is mounted on a powerful horse, I would suggest that he should each time ride round on the outer flank; in which case he will himself be kept perpetually moving at a canter, and those with him, as they become the wheeling flank, will, by turns, fall into the same pace, with this result: the spectacle presented to the senate will be that of an ever rapidly moving stream of cavaliers; and the horses having, each in turn, the opportunity to recover breath, will not be overdone.

[14] {dokimasiais}, reviews and inspections. See A. Martin, op. cit. p. 333.

[15] Where? Some think in a lost passage of the work (see Courier, p. 111, n. 1); or is the reference to ch. ii. above? and is the scene of the {dokimasiai} Phaleron? There is no further refernece to {ta Phaleroi}. Cf. S. 1, above. See Aristot. "Ath. Pol." 49 (now the locus classicus on the subject), and Dr. Sandys ad loc. The scene is represented on a patera from Orvieto, now in the Berlin Museum, reproduced and fully described in "The Art of Horsemanship by Xenophon," translated, with chapters on the Greek Riding–Horse, and with notes, by Morris H. Morgan, p. 76.

On occasions when the display takes place in the hippodrome,[16] the best arrangement would be, in the first place, that the troops should fill the entire space with extended front, so forcing out the mob of people from the centre;[17] and secondly, that in the sham fight[18] which ensues, the tribal squadrons, swiftly pursuing and retiring, should gallop right across and through each other, the two hipparchs at their head, each with five squadrons under him. Consider the effect of such a spectacle: the grim advance of rival squadrons front to front; the charge; the solemn pause as, having swept across the hippodrome, they stand once more confronting one another; and then the trumpet sounds, whereat a second and yet swifter hostile advance, how fine the effect!—and once again they are at the halt; and once again the trumpet sounds, and for the third time, at the swiftest pace of all, they make a final charge across the field, before dismissal; after which they come to a halt en masse, in battle order; and, as now customary,[19] ride up to salute the senate, and disband. These evolutions will at once approve themselves, I think, not only for their novelty, but for their resemblacne to real warfare. The notion that the hipparch is to ride at a slower pace than his phylarchs, and to handle his horse precisely in their style, seems to me below the dignity of the office.

[16] In the hippodrome near Munychia, I suppose.

[17] Lit. ". . . it would be beautiful to form with extended front, so as to fill the hippodrome with horses and drive out the people from the central space, beautiful to . . ." The new feature of the review would seem to have been the introduction of a sham fight in three parts, down to the customary advance of the whole corps, {epi phalaggos}. Cf. Virg. "Aen." v. 545 foll. But see Martin, op. cit. 197.

[18] Lit. "the anthippasia."

[19] "As is your custom." See "Mem." III. iii. 6.

When the cavalry parade takes place on the hard–trodden[20] ground of the Academy, I have the following advice to give. To avoid being jolted off his horse at any moment, the trooper should, in charging, lean well back,[21] and to prevent his charger stumbling, he should while wheeling hold his head well up, but along a straight stretch he should force the pace. Thus the spectacle presented to the senate will combine the elements of beauty and of safety.

[20] Cf. Thuc. vii. 27.

[21] See "Horsemanship," vii. 17.

IV

To pass to a different topic: on the march, the general will need to exercise a constant forethought to relieve the horses' backs and the troopers' legs, by a judicious interchange of riding and of marching. Wherein consists the golden mean, will not be hard to find;

since "every man a standard to himself,"[1] applies, and your sensations are an index to prevent your fellows being overdone through inadvertence.

[1] The phrase is proverbial. Cf. Plat. "Theaet." 183 B.

But now supposing you are on the march in some direction, and it is uncertain whether you will stumble on the enemy, your duty is to rest your squadrons in turn; since it will go hard with you, if the enemy come to close quarters when the whole force is dismounted.[2] Or, again, suppose the roads are narrow, or you have to cross a defile, you will pass, by word of mouth, the command to diminish the front;[3] or given, again, you are debouching on broad roads, again the word of command will pass by word of mouth, to every squadron, "to increase their front"; or lastly, supposing you have reached flat country, "to form squadron in order of battle." If only for the sake of practice, it is well to go through evolutions of the sort;[4] besides which it adds pleasure to the march thus to diversify the line of route with cavalry mavouvres.

[2] See "Hell." V. iv. 40 for a case in point.

[3] Or, "advance by column of route." See "Hell." VII. iv. 23.

[4] Or, "it is a pleasant method of beguiling the road." Cf. Plat.
    "Laws," i. 625 B.

Supposing, however, you are off roads altogether and moving fast over difficult ground, no matter whether you are in hostile or in friendly territory, it will be useful if the scouts attached to squadrons[5] rode on in advance, their duty being, in case of encountering pathless clefts or gullies, to work round on to practicable ground, and to discover at what point the troopers may effect a passage, so that whole ranks may not go blindly roaming.[6]

[5] {ton upereton} = "ground scouts," al. "orderlies." Ordonnances,
    trabans (Courier). See Rustow and Kochly, p. 140. "Cyrop." II. i.
    21; II. iv. 4; V. iii. 52; VII. v. 18, and VI. ii. 13; "Anab." I.
    ix. 27; II. i. 9; where "adjutants," "orderlies" would seem to be
    implied.

[6] Al. "to prevent whole divisions losing their way." Cf. "Anab."
   VIII. iii. 18.

Again, if there is prospect of danger on the march, a prudent general can hardly show his wisdom better than by sending out advanced patrols in front of the ordinary exploring parties to reconnoitre every inch of ground minutely. So to be apprised of the enemy's position in advance, and at as great a distance off as possible, cannot fail to be useful, whether for purposes of attack or defence; just as it is useful also to enforce a halt at the passage of a river or some other defile, so that the men in rear may not knock their horses all to bits in endeavouring to overtake their leader. These are precepts known, I admit, to nearly all the world, but it is by no means every one who will take pains to apply them carefully.[7]

[7] See "Econ." xx. 6. foll.

It is the business of the hipparch to take infinite precautions while it is still peace, to make himself acquainted with the details, not only of his own, but of the hostile territory;[8] or if, as may well betide, he personally should lack the knowledge, he should invite the aid of others[9]—those best versed in the topography of any district. Since there is all the difference in the world between a leader acquainted with his roads and one who is not; and when it comes to actual designs upon the enemy, the difference between knowing and not knowing the locality can hardly be exaggerated.

[8] Or, "with hostile and friendly territories alike."

[9] Lit. "he should associate with himself those of the rest"; i.e.
   his colleagues or other members of the force.

So, too, with regard to spies and intelligencers. Before war commences your business is to provide yourself with a supply of people friendly to both states, or maybe merchants (since states are ready to receive the importer of goods with open arms); sham deserters may be found occasionally useful.[10] Not, of course, that the confidence you feel in your spies must ever cause you to neglect outpost duty; indeed your state of preparation should at any moment be precisely what it ought to be, supposing the approach or the imminent arrival of the enemy were to be announced. Let a spy be ever so faithful, there is always the risk he may fail to report his intelligence at the critical moment, since the obstacles which present themselves in war are not to be counted on the fingers.

[10] Cf. "Cyrop." VI. i. 39, where one of the Persians, Araspas,
   undertakes to play this role to good effect.

But to proceed to another topic. The enemy is less likely to get wind of an advance of cavalry, if the orders for march were passed from mouth to mouth rather than announced by voice of herald, or public notice.[11] Accordingly, in addition to[12] this method of ordering the march by word passed along the line, the appointment of file– leaders seems desirable, who again are to be supplemented by section– leaders,[13] so that the number of men to whom each petty officer has to transmit an order will be very few;[14] while the section–leaders will deploy and increase the front, whatever the formation, without confusion, whenever there is occasion for the movement.[15]

[11] i.e. "given by general word of command, or in writing." As to the
   "word–of–mouth command," see above, S. 3; "Hell." VII. v. 9; and
   for the "herald," see "Anab." III. iv. 36.

[12] Reading {pros to dia p.}, or if {pros to} . . . transl. "with a
   view to."

[13] Lit. pempadarchs, i.e. No. 6 in the file. See "Cyrop." II. i. 22
   foll., iii. 21.

[14] Lit. "so that each officer may pass the word to as few as
   possible."

[15] Cf. "Anab." IV. vi. 6.

When an advanced guard is needed, I say for myself I highly approve of secret pickets and outposts, if only because in supplying a guard to protect your friends you are contriving an ambuscade to catch the enemy. Also the outposts will be less exposed to a secret attack, being themselves unseen, and yet a source of great alarm to the enemy; since the bare knowledge that there are outposts somewhere, though where precisely no man knows, will prevent the enemy from feeling confident, and oblige him to mistrust every tenable position. An exposed outpost, on the contrary, presents to the broad eye of day its dangers and also its weaknesses.[16] Besides which, the holder of a concealed outpost can always place a few exposed vedettes beyond his hidden pickets, and so endeavour to decoy the enemy into an ambuscade. Or he may play the part of trapper with effect by placing a second exposed outpost in rear of the other; a device which may serve to take in the unwary foeman quite as well as that before named.

[16] Lit. "makes plain its grounds of terror as of confidence."

Indeed I take it to be the mark of a really prudent general never to run a risk of his own choosing, except where it is plain to him beforehand, that he will get the better of his adversary. To play into the enemy's hands may more fitly be described as treason to one's fellow—combatants than true manliness. So, too, true generalship consists in attacking where the enemy is weakest, even if the point be some leagues distant. Severity of toil weighs nothing in the scale against the danger of engaging a force superior to your own.[17] Still, if on any occasion the enemy advance in any way to place himself between fortified points that are friendly to you, let him be never so superior in force, your game is to attack on whichever flank you can best conceal your advance, or, still better, on both flanks simultaneously; since, while one detachment is retiring after delivering its attack, a charge pressed home from the opposite quarter cannot fail to throw the enemy into confusion and to give safety to your friends.

[17] N.B. Throughout this treatise the author has to meet the case of
    a small force of cavalry acting on the defensive.

How excellent a thing it is to endeavour to ascertain an enemy's position by means of spies and so forth, as in ancient story; yet best of all, in my opinion, is it for the commander to try to seize some coign of vantage, from which with his own eyes he may descry the movements of the enemy and watch for any error on his part.[18]

[18] As, e.g. Epaminondas at Tegea. See "Hell." VII. v. 9.

Whatever may be snatched by ruse, thief fashion,[19] your business is to send a competent patrol to seize; or again where capture by coup de main[20] is practicable, you will despatch a requisite body of troops to effect a coup de main. Or take the case: the enemy is on the march in some direction, and a portion of his force becomes detached from his main body or through excess of confidence is caught straggling; do not let the opportunity escape, but make it a rule always to pursue a weaker with a stronger force.[21] These, indeed, are rules of procedure, which it only requires a simple effort of the mind to appreciate. Creatures far duller of wit than man have this ability: kites and falcons, when anything is left unguarded, pounce and carry it off and retire into safety without being caught; or wolves, again, will hunt down any quarry left widowed of its guard, or thieve what they can in darksome corners.[22] In case a dog pursues and overtakes them, should he chance to be weaker the wolf attacks him, or if stronger, the wolf will slaughter[23] his quarry and make off. At other times, if the pack be strong enough to make light of the guardians of a flock, they will marshal their battalions, as it were, some to drive off the guard and others to effect the capture, and so by stealth or fair fight they provide themselves with the necessaries of life. I say, if dumb beasts are capable of conducting a raid with so much sense and skill, it is hard if any average man cannot prove himself equally intelligent with creatures which themselves fall victims to the craft of man.

[19] e.g. defiles, bridges, outposts, stores, etc.

[20] e.g. a line of outposts, troops in billets or bivouac, etc.

[21] "It is a maxim, the quarry should be weaker than the pursuer."

[22] Zeune cf. Ael. "N. A." viii. 14, on the skill of wolves in hunting.

[23] For {aposphaxas} Courier suggests {apospasas}, "dragging off what he can."

V

Here is another matter which every horseman ought to know, and that is within what distance a horse can overhaul a man on foot; or the interval necessary to enable a slower horse to escape one more fleet. It is the business rather of the cavalry general to recognise at a glance the sort of ground on which infantry will be superior to cavalry and where cavalry will be superior to infantry. He should be a man of invention, ready of device to turn all circumstances to account, so as to give at one time a small body of cavalry the appearance of a larger, and again a large the likeness of a smaller body; he should have the craft to appear absent when close at hand, and within striking distance when a long way off; he should know exactly not only how to steal an enemy's position, but by a master stroke of cunning[1] to spirit his own cavalry away, and, when least expected, deliver his attack. Another excellent specimen of inventiveness may be seen in the general's ability, while holding a weak position himself, to conjure up so lively an apprehension in the enemy that he will not dream of attacking; or conversely, when, being in a strong position himself, he can engender a fatal boldness in the adversary to venture an attack. Thus with the least cost to yourself, you will best be able to catch your enemy tripping.

[1] Or, "sleight of hand"; and for {kleptein} = escamoter see "Anab."
   IV. vi. 11, 15; V. vi. 9.

But to avoid suspicion of seeming to prescribe impossible feats, I will set down, in so many words, the procedure in certain crucial instances.

The best safeguard against failure in any attempt to enforce pursuit or conduct a retreat lies in a thorough knowledge of your horse's powers.[2] But how is this experience to be got? Simply by paying attention to their behaviour in the peaceable manouvres of the sham fight, when there is no real enemy to intervene—how the animals come off, in fact, and what stamina they show in the various charges and retreats.

[2] {empeiria}, "empirical knowledge."

Or suppose the problem is to make your cavalry appear numerous. In the first place, let it be a fundamental rule, if possible, not to attempt to delude the enemy at close quarters; distance, as it aids illusion, will promote security. The next point is to bear in mind that a mob of horses clustered together (owing perhaps to the creatures' size) will give a suggestion of number, whereas scattered they may easily be counted.

Another means by which you may give your troop an appearance of numerical strength beyond reality consists in posting, in and out between the troopers, so many lines of grooms[3] who should carry lances if possible, or staves at any rate to look like lances—a plan which will serve alike whether you mean to display your cavalry force at the halt or are deploying to increase front; in either case, obviously the bulk and volume of the force, whatever your formation, will appear increased. Conversely, if the problem be to make large numbers appear small, supposing you have ground at command adapted to concealment, the thing is simple: by leaving a portion of your men exposed and hiding away a portion in obscurity, you may effect your object.[4] But if the ground nowhere admits of cover, your best course is to form your files[5] into ranks one behind the other, and wheel them round so as to leave intervals between each file; the troopers nearest the enemy in each file will keep their lances erect, and the rest low enough not to show above.

[3] Cf. Polyaen. II. i. 17, of Agesilaus in Macedonia, 394 B.C. (our author was probably present); IV. iv. 3, of Antipater in Thessaly, 323 B.C.

[4] Lit. "steal your troopers." See "Cyrop." V. iv. 48.

[5] Lit. "form your decads (squads of ten; cf. our 'fours') in ranks and deploy with intervals."

To come to the next topic: you may work on the enemy's fears by the various devices of mock ambuscades, sham relief parties, false information. Conversely, his confidence will reach an overweening pitch, if the idea gets abroad that his opponents have troubles of their own and little leisure for offensive operations.

But over and beyond all that can be written on the subject— inventiveness is a personal matter, beyond all formulas—the true general must be able to take in, deceive, decoy, delude his adversary at every turn, as the particular occasion demands. In fact, there is no instrument of war more cunning than chicanery;[6] which is not surprising when one reflects that even little boys, when playing, "How many (marbles) have I got in my hand?"[7] are able to take one another in successfully. Out goes a clenched fist, but with such cunning that he who holds a few is thought to hold several; or he may present several and appear to be holding only a few. Is it likely that a grown man, giving his whole mind to methods of chicanery, will fail of similar inventiveness? Indeed, when one comes to consider what is meant by advantages snatched in war, one will find, i think, that the greater part of them, and those the more important, must be attributed in some way or other to displays of craft;[8] which things being so, a man had better either not attempt to exercise command, or, as part and parcel of his general equipment, let him pray to Heaven to enable him to exercise this faculty and be at pains himself to cultivate his own inventiveness.

[6] Cf. "Cyrop." IV. ii. 26; VII. i. 18.

[7] {posinda}, lit. "How many?" (i.e. dice, nuts, marbles, etc.); cf. the old game, "Buck! buck! how many horns do I hold up?" Schneid. cf. Aristot. "Rhet."iii. 5. 4.

[8] "Have been won in connection with craft." See "Cyrop." I. vi. 32; "Mem." III. i. 6; IV. ii. 15.

A general, who has access to the sea, may exercise the faculty as follows: he may either, whilst apparently engaged in fitting out his vessels, strike a blow on land;[9] or with a make-believe of some aggressive design by land, hazard an adventure by sea.[10]

[9] A ruse adopted by Jason, 371 B.C. Cf. "Hell." VI. iv. 21.

[10] Cf. the tactics of the Athenians at Catana, 415 B.C. Thuc. vi. 64.

I consider it to be the duty of the cavalry commander to point out clearly to the state authority the essential weakness of a force of cavalry unaided by light infantry, as opposed to cavalry with foot- soldiers attached.[11] It is duty also, having got his footmen, to turn the force to good account. It is possible to conceal them effectively, not only between the lines, but in rear also of the troopers—the mounted soldier towering high above his follower on foot.

[11] Or, "divorced from infantry." In reference to {amippoi}, cf. Thuc. v. 57; "Hell." VII. v. 23.

With regard to these devices and to any others which invention may suggest towards capturing the foeman by force or fraud, I have one common word of advice to add, which is, to act with God, and then while Heaven propitious smiles, fortune will scarcely dare to frown.[12]

[12] Or, "and then by the grace of Heaven you may win the smiles of
   fortune," reading with Courier, etc., {ina kai e tukhe sunepaine}.
   Cf. "Cyrop." III. iii. 20.

At times there is no more effective fraud than a make–believe[13] of over–caution alien
to the spirit of adventure. This itself will put the enemy off his guard and ten to one will
lure him into some egregious blunder; or conversely, once get a reputation for
foolhardiness established, and then with folded hands sit feigning future action, and see
what a world of trouble you will thereby cause your adversary.

[13] S. 15 should perhaps stand before S. 13.

VI

But, after all, no man, however great his plastic skill, can hope to mould and shape a
work of art to suit his fancy, unless the stuff on which he works be first prepared and
made ready to obey the craftsman's will. Nor certainly where the raw material consists of
men, will you succeed, unless, under God's blessing, these same men have been prepared
and made ready to meet their officer in a friendly spirit. They must come to look upon
him as of greater sagacity than themselves in all that concerns encounter with the enemy.
This friendly disposition on the part of his subordinates, one must suppose, will best be
fostered by a corresponding sympathy on the part of their commander towards the men
themselves, and that not by simple kindness but by the obvious pains he takes on their
behalf, at one time to provide them with food, and at another to secure safety of retreat, or
again by help of outposts and the like, to ensure protection during rest and sleep.

When on active service[1] the commander must prove himself conspicuously careful in
the matter of forage, quarters, water–supply, outposts,[2] and all other requisites;
forecasting the future and keeping ever a wakeful eye in the interest of those under him;
and in case of any advantage won, the truest gain which the head of affairs can reap is to
share with his men the profits of success.

[1] Al. "on garrison outpost duty."

[2] Reading {phulakon}, or if with Courier {thulakon}, "haversacks,"

i.e. "la farine, le contenant pour le contenu."

Indeed, to put the matter in a nutshell, there is small risk a general will be regarded with contempt by those he leads, if, whatever he may have to preach, he shows himself best able to perform.

Beginning with the simple art of mounting on horseback, let him so train himself in all particulars of horsemanship that, to look at him, the men must see their leader is a horseman who can leap a trench unscathed or scale a parapet,[3] or gallop down a bank, and hurl a javelin with the best. These are accomplishments which one and all will pave the way to make contempt impossible. If, further, the men shall see in their commander one who, with the knowledge how to act, has force of will and cunning to make them get the better of the enemy; and if, further, they have got the notion well into their heads that this same leader may be trusted not to lead them recklesssly against the foe, without the help of Heaven, or despite the auspices— I say, you have a list of virtues which will make those under his command the more obedient to their ruler.

[3] Or, "stone walls," "dykes."

VII

If prudence may be spoken of as the one quality distinctive of true generalship, there are two respects in which a general of cavalry at Athens should pre–eminently excel. Not only must he show a dutiful submission to the gods; but he must possess great fighting qualities, seeing that he has on his borders a rival cavalry equal to his own in number and backed by a large force of heavy infantry.[1] So that, if he undertake to invade the enemy's territory unsupported by the other forces of the city[2]—in dealing with two descriptions of forces single–handed, he and his cavalry must look for a desperate adventure; or to take the converse case, that the enemy invades the soil of Attica, to begin with, he will not invade at all, unless supported by other cavalry besides his own and an infantry force sufficient to warrant the supposition that no force on our side can cope with him.

[1] The reference is doubtless to the Thebans. Unfortunately we do not
   know, on good authority, how many troops of either arm they had in

the field at Leuctra or at Mantinea.

[2] Lit. "without the rest of the city," i.e. the hoplites, etc.

Now, to deal with this vast hostile array, if only the city will determine to sally out en masse to protect her rural districts, the prospect is fair. Under God, our troopers, if properly cared for, are the finer men; our infantry of the line are no less numerous, and as regards physique, if it comes to that, not one whit inferior, while in reference to moral qualities, they are more susceptible to the spur of a noble ambition, if only under God's will they be correctly trained. Or again, as touching pride of ancestry, what have Athenians to fear as against Boeotians on that score?[3]

[3] See "Mem." III. v. 3, where it is contended that in pride of
    ancestry Athenians can hold their own against Boeotians.

But suppose the city of Athens determine to betake herself to her navy, as in the old days when the Lacedaemonians, leagued with the rest of Hellas, brought invasion;[4] and is content once more simply to protect her walls through thick and thin. As to protecting what lies outside the city wall she looks to her cavalry for that; and single−handed her troopers must do desperate encounter against the united forces of the enemy. I say, under these circumstances, we shall need in the first place the strong support of Heaven; and in the second place, well will it be for us if our cavalry commander prove himself a consummate officer.[5] Indeed, he will have need of large wisdom to deal with a force so vastly superior in numbers, and of enterprise to strike when the critical moment comes.

[4] See Thuc. ii. 13, 14, 22, etc., and in particular iv. 95,
    Hippocrates' speech before the battle of Delium, 424 B.C.

[5] A "parfait marechal."

He must also, as it appears to me, be capable of great physical endurance;[6] since clearly, if he has to run full tilt against an armament present, as we picture, in such force that not even our whole state cares to cope with it, it is plain he must accept whatever fate is due, where might is right, himself unable to retaliate.

[6] So Jason, "Hell." VI. i. 4.

If, on the contrary, he elect to guard the territory outside the walls[7] with a number just sufficient to keep a look–out on the enemy, and to withdraw into safe quarters from a distance whatever needs protection—a small number, be it observed, is just as capable of vedette duty, as well able, say, to scan the distant horizon, as a large; and by the same token men with no great confidence in themselves or in their horses are not ill–qualified to guard, or withdraw within shelter[8] the property of friends; since fear, as the proverb has it, makes a shrewd watchman. The proposal, therefore, to select from these a corps of observation will most likely prove true strategy. But what then of the residue not needed for outpost duty? If any one imagines he has got an armament, he will find it miserably small, and lacking in every qualification necessary to risk an open encounter.

[7] Or, "His better plan would be to."

[8] Reading {anakhorizein}. Cf. "Cyrop." II. ii. 8; "Anab." V. ii. 10;
   or if {anakhorein eis}, transl. "or retire into safe quarters."
   See "Hell." IV. vi. 44.

But let him make up his mind to employ it in guerilla war, and he will find the force quite competent for that, I warrant. His business, so at least it seems to me, will be to keep his men perpetually in readiness to strike a blow, and without exposing himself, to play sentinel, waiting for any false move on the part of the hostile armament. And it is a way with soldiers, bear in mind, the more numerous they are, the more blunders they commit. They must needs scatter of set purpose[9] in search of provisions; or through the disorder incidental to a march, some will advance and others lag behind, beyond a proper limit. Blunders like these, then, our hipparch must not let pass unpunished (unless he wishes the whole of Attica to become a gigantic camp);[10] keeping his single point steadily in view, that when he strikes a blow he must be expeditious and retire before the main body has time to rally to the rescue.

[9] {epimeleia}. Cf. "Cyrop." V. iii. 47.

[10] Lit. "or else the whole of Attica will be one encampment." As at
   the date of the fortification of Decelea (413 B.C.), which
   permanently commanded the whole country. See Thuc. vii. 27. Al.
   Courier, "autrement vous n'avez plus de camp, ou pour mieux dire,
   tout le pays devient votre camp."

Again, it frequently happens on the march, that an army will get into roads where numbers are no advantage. Again, in the passage of rivers, defiles, and the like, it is possible for a general with a head on his shoulders to hang on the heels of an enemy in security, and to determine with precision[11] the exact number of the enemy he will care to deal with. Occasionally the fine chance occurs to atack the foe while encamping or breakfasting or supping, or as the men turn out of bed: seasons at which the soldier is apt to be unharnessed—the hoplite for a shorter, the cavalry trooper for a longer period.[12]

[11] See "Anab." II. v. 18; "Cyrop." III. iii. 47; IV. i. 18.
{tamieusasthai}, "with the precision of a controller."

[12] Cf. "Hell." II. iv. 6; VII. i. 16.

As to vedettes and advanced outposts, you should never cease planning and plotting against them. For these in their turn, as a rule, are apt to consist of small numbers, and are sometimes posted at a great distance from their own main body. But if after all it turns out that the enemy are well on their guard against all such attempts, then, God helping, it would be a feat of arms to steal into the enemy's country, first making it your business to ascertain[13] his defences, the number of men at this, that, and the other point, and how they are distributed throughout the country. For there is no booty so splendid as an outpost so overmastered; and these frontier outposts are especially prone to be deceived, with their propensity to give chase to any small body they set eyes on, regarding that as their peculiar function. You will have to see, however, in retiring that your line of retreat is not right into the jaws of the enemy's reliefs hastening to the scene of action.

[13] Or, "having first studied." Cf. "Mem." III. vi. 10.

VIII

It stands to reason, however, that in order to be able to inflict real damage upon a greatly superior force, the weaker combatant must possess such a moral superiority over the other as shall enable him to appear in the position of an expert, trained in all the feats of cavalry performance in the field, and leave his enemy to play the part of raw recruits or amateurs.[1]

The Cavalry General

[1] Cf. "Cyrop." I. v. 11; "Mem." III. vii. 7.

And this end may be secured primarily on this wise: those who are to form your guerilla bands[2] must be so hardened and inured to the saddle that they are capable of undergoing all the toils of a campaign.[3] That a squadron (and I speak of horse and man alike) should enter these lists in careless, disorderly fashion suggests the idea of a troop of women stepping into the arena to cope with male antagonists.

[2] Or, add, "for buccaneers and free-lances you must be."

[3] Lit. "every toil a soldier can encounter."

But reverse the picture. Suppose men and horses to have been taught and trained to leap trenches and scale dykes, to spring up banks, and plunge from heights without scathe, to gallop headlong at full speed adown a steep: they will tower over unpractised opponents as the birds of the air tower over creatures that crawl and walk.[4] Their feet are case-hardened by constant training, and, when it comes to tramping over rough ground, must differ from the uninitiated as the sound man from the lame. And so again, when it comes to charging and retiring, the onward-dashing gallop, the well-skilled, timely retreat, expert knowledge of the ground and scenery will assert superiority over inexpertness like that of eyesight over blindness.

[4] See "Horse." viii. 6; cf. "Hunting," xii. 2; "Cyrop." I. vi. 28
  foll.

Nor should it be forgotten, that in order to be in thorough efficiency the horses must not only be well fed and in good condition, but at the same time so seasoned by toil that they will go through their work without the risk of becoming broken-winded. And lastly, as bits and saddle-cloths (to be efficient)[5] need to be attached by straps, a cavalry general should never be without a good supply, whereby at a trifling expense he may convert a number of nonplussed troopers into serviceable fighting men.[6]

[5] [{khresima}] L.D. For the {upomnema} itself cf. "Cyrop." VI. ii.
  32.

[6] Or, "thus at a trifling outlay he will be able to render so many
non-efficients useful." Al. "make the articles as good as new."

But if any one is disposed to dwell on the amount of trouble it will cost him, if he is
required to devote himself to horsemanship so assiduously, let him console himself with
the reflection that the pains and labours undergone by any man in training for a
gymnastic contest are far larger and more formidable than any which the severest training
of the horseman will involve; and for this reason, that the greater part of gymnastic
exercises are performed "in the sweat of the brow," while equestrian exercise is
performed with pleasure. Indeed, there is no accomplishment which so nearly realises the
aspiration of a man to have the wings of a bird than this of horsemanship.[7] But further,
to a victory obtained in war attaches a far greater weight of glory than belongs to the
noblest contest of the arena.[8] Of these the state indeed will share her meed of glory,[9]
but in honour of victory in war the very gods are wont to crown whole states with
happiness.[10] So that, for my part, I know not if there be aught else which has a higher
claim to be practised than the arts of war.

[7] Cf. "Cyrop." IV. iii. 15; Herod. iv. 132; Plat. "Rep." v. 467 D.

[8] Cf. Eur. "Autolycus," fr. 1, trans. by J. A. Symonds, "Greek
Poets," 2nd series, p. 283.

[9] Cf. Plut. "Pelop." 34 (Clough, ii. p. 235): "And yet who would
compare all the victories in the Pythian and Olympian games put
together, with one of these enterprises of Pelopidas, of which he
successfully performed so many?"

[10] "To bind about the brows of states happiness as a coronal."

And this, too, is worth noting: that the buccaneer by sea, the privateersman, through long
practice in endurance, is able to live at the expense of far superior powers. Yes, and the
life of the freebooter is no less natural and appropriate to landsmen—I do not say, to
those who can till and gather in the fruit of their fields, but to those who find themselves
deprived of sustenance; since there is no alternative—either men must till their fields or
live on the tillage of others, otherwise how will they find the means either of living or of
obtaining peace?[11]

The Cavalry General

[11] Cf. "Econ." v. 7.

Here, too, is a maxim to engrave upon the memory: in charging a superior force, never to leave a difficult tract of ground in the rear of your attack, since there is all the difference in the world between a stumble in flight and a stumble in pursuit.

There is another precaution which I feel called upon to note. Some generals,[12] in attacking a force which they imagine to be inferior to their own, will advance with a ridiculously insufficient force,[13] so that it is the merest accident if they do not experience the injury they were minded to inflict. Conversely, in attacking any enemy whose superiority is a well-known fact, they will bring the whole of their force into action.

[12] Or, "one knows of generals," e.g. Iphicrates at Oneion, 369 B.C.
    Cf. "Hell." VI. v. 51.

[13] Lit. "an absolutely weak force."

Now, my maxim would be precisely converse: if you attack with a prospect of superiority, do not grudge employing all the power at your command; excess of victory[14] never yet caused any conqueror one pang of remorse.

[14] Or, "a great and decided victory." Cf. "Hiero," ii. 16.

But in any attempt to attack superior forces, in full certainty that, do what you can, you must eventually retire, it is far better, say I, under these circumstances to bring a fraction only of your whole force into action, which fraction should be the pick and flower of the troops at your command, both horses and men. A body of that size and quality will be able to strike a blow and to fall back with greater security. Whereas, if a general brings all his troops into action against a superior force, when he wishes to retire, certain things must happen: those of his men who are worse mounted will be captured, others through lack of skill in horsemanship will be thrown, and a third set be cut off owing to mere difficulties of ground; since it is impossible to find any large tract of country exactly what you would desire. If for no other reason, through sheer stress of numbers there will be collisions, and much damage done by kicks through mutual entanglement; whereas a pick of horse and men will be able to escape offhand,[15] especially if you have invention to create a scare in the minds of the pursuers by help of the moiety of troops who are out of action.[16] For this purpose false ambuscades will be of use.

[15] Or, "by themselves," reading {ex auton}, as L. Dind. suggests.
   Cf. Polyb. x. 40. 6, or if as vulg. {ex auton} (sub. {kheiron},
   Weiske), transl. "to slip through their fingers."

[16] Zeune and other commentators cf Liv. v. 38 (Diod. xiv. 114), but
   the part played by the Roman subsidiarii at the battle of the
   Allia, if indeed "una salus fugientibus," was scarcely happy.
   Would not "Hell." VII. v. 26 be more to the point? The detachment
   of cavalry and infantry placed by Epaminondas "on certain crests,
   to create an apprehension in the minds of the Athenians" in that
   quarter of the field at Mantinea was a {mekhanema} of the kind
   here contemplated.

Another serviceable expedient will be to discover on which side a friendly force may suddenly appear and without risk to itself put a drag on the wheels of the pursuer. Nay, it is self–evident, I think, that, as far as work and speed are concerned, it is the small body which will assert its superiority more rapidly over the larger, and not vice versa—not of course that the mere fact of being a small body will enable them to endure toil or give them wings; but simply it is easier to find five men than five hundred, who will take the requisite care and pains with their horses, and personally practise of their own accord the art of horsemanship.

But suppose the chance should occur of entering the lists against an equal number of the enemy's cavalry, according to my judgment it were no bad plan to split the squadron into divisions,[17] the first of which should be commanded by the squadron–leader, and the other by the ablest officer to be found. This second–officer will for the time being follow in rear of the leading division with the squadron leader; and by and by, when the antagonist is in near proximity, and when the word of command is passed, form squadron to the front and charge the hostile ranks[18]—a manouvre calculated, as I conceive, to bring the whole mass down upon the enemy with paralysing force, and to cause him some trouble to extricate himself. Ideally speaking, both divisions[19] will be backed by infantry kept in rear of the cavalry; these will suddenly disclose themselves, and rushing to close quarters, in all probability clench the nail of victory.[20] So at any rate it strikes

33

me, seeing as I do the effects of what is unexpected— how, in the case of good things, the soul of man is filled to overflowing with joy, and again, in the case of things terrible, paralysed with amazement. In proof of what I say, let any one reflect on the stupor into which a body of men with all the weight of numerical advantage on their side will be betrayed by falling into an ambuscade; or again, on the exaggerated terror mutually inspired in belligerents during the first few days, of finding themselves posted in face of one another.

[17] Or, "troops."

[18] Possibly on flank. See Courier, p. 35, on Spanish cavalry
    tactics.

[19] Lit. "supposing both divisions to be backed by footmen," etc.

[20] Or, "achieve a much more decisive victory." Cf. "Cyrop." III.
    iii. 28.

To make these dispositions is not hard; the difficulty is to discover a body of men who will dash forward[21] and charge an enemy as above described intelligently and loyally, with an eager spirit and unfailing courage. That is a problem for a good cavalry general to solve. I mean an officer who must be competent to so assert himself in speech or action[22] that those under him will no longer hesitate. They will recognise of themselves that it is a good thing and a right to obey,[23] to follow their leader, to rush to close quarters with the foe. A desire will consume them to achieve some deed of glory and renown. A capacity will be given them patiently to abide by the resolution of their souls.

[21] {parelontas}, in reference to S. 18 above, {parelaunoi}, "form
    squadron to the front."

[22] "To be this, he must be able as an orator as well as a man of
    action." Cf. "Mem." II. ii. 11.

[23] Cf. Tennyson's "The Charge of the Light Brigade":

Their's not to make reply, Their's not to reason why, Their's but to do and die.

To turn to another matter, take the case in which you have two armeis facing one another in battle order, or a pair of fortresses[24] belonging to rival powers, and in the space between all kinds of cavalry manouvres are enacted, wheelings and charges and retreats.[25] Under such circumstances the custom usually is for either party after wheeling to set off at a slow pace and to gallop full speed only in the middle of the course. But now suppose that a commander, after making feint[26] in this style, presently on wheeling quickens for the charge and quickens to retire—he will be able to hit the enemy far harder, and pull through absolutely without scathe himself most likely; through charging at full speed whilst in proximity to his own stronghold (or main body), and quickening to a gallop as he retires from the stronghold (or main body) of the enemy. If further, he could secretly contrive to leave behind four or five troopers, the bravest and best mounted of the squadron, it would give them an immense advantage in falling upon the enemy whilst wheeling to return to the charge.[27]

[24] Al. "fields and farmsteads between."

[25] Or, "retirements," see "Horsemanship," viii. 12; "Cyrop." V. iv. 8; "Hell." IV. ii. 6; "Ages." ii. 3.

[26] Or, "having precluded in this fashion. See Theocr. xxii. 102:

{ton men anax ataraxen etosia khersi prodeiknus Pantothen},

"feinting on every side" (A. Lang). Al. "having given due warning of his intention." Cf. Aristot. "H. A." ix. 37.

[27] Cf. Aristoph. "Knights," 244 (Demosthenes calls to the hipparchs[?]):

{andres eggus . all' amunou, kapanastrephou palin}.

IX

To read these observations over a few times will be sufficient, but for giving them effect the officer will need perpetually to act as circumstances require.[1] He must take in the situation at a glance, and carry out unflinchingly whatever is expedient for the moment. To set down in writing everything that he must do, is not a whit more possible than to know the future as a whole.[2] But of all hints and suggestions the most important to my mind is this: whatever you determine to be right, with diligence endeavour to perform. For be it tillage of the soil, or trading, or seafaring, or the art of ruling, without pains applied to bring the matter to perfection, the best theories in the world, the most correct conclusions, will be fruitless.

[1] {pros to paratugkhanon}, lit. "to meet emergencies." Cf. Thuc. i.
122: "For war, least of all things, conforms to prescribed rules;
it strikes out a path for itself when the moment comes" (Jowett).

[2] Or, "is about as feasible as to foretell each contingency hid in
the womb of futurity."

One thing I am prepared to insist on: it is clear to myself that by Heaven's help our total cavalry force might be much more quickly raised to the full quota of a thousand troopers,[3] and with far less friction to the mass of citizens, by the enrolment of two hundred foreign cavalry. Their acquisition will be doubly helpful, as intensifying the loyalty of the entire force and as kindling a mutual ambition to excel in manly virtue.

[3] See Schneid. ad loc.; Boeckh, "P. E. A." pp. 263, 264; Herod. vi.
112; Thuc. vi. 31; Aristoph. "Knights," 223; Aeschin. "De F. L."
334–337. See for this reform, Martin, op. cit. 343, 368.

I can state on my own knowledge that the Lacedaemonian cavalry only began to be famous[4] with the introduction of foreign troopers; and in the other states of Hellas everywhere the foreign brigades stand in high esteem, as I perceive. Need, in fact, contributes greatly to enthusiasm. Towards the necessary cost of the horses I hold that an ample fund will be provided,[5] partly out of the pockets of those who are only too glad to escape cavalry service (in other words, those on whom the service devolves prefer to pay a sum of money down and be quit of the duty),[6] and from wealthy men who are physically incompetent; and I do not see why orphans possessed of large estates should not contribute.[7] Another belief I hold is that amongst our resident aliens[8] there are some who will show a laudable ambition if incorporated with the cavalry. I argue from the fact, apparent to myself, that amongst this class persons are to be found most zealously disposed to carry out the part assigned to them, in every other branch of honourable service which the citizens may choose to share with them. Again, it strikes me that if you seek for an energetic infantry to support your cavalry, you will find it in a corps composed of individuals whose hatred to the foe is naturally intense.[9] But the success of the above suggestions will depend doubtless on the consenting will of Heaven.[10]

[4] "Entered on an era of prestige with the incorporation of," after
   Leuctra, 371 B.C., when the force was at its worst. See "Hell."
   VI. iv. 10.

[5] Or, "money will be forthcoming for them." Cf. Lys. "Against
   Philon," xxxi. 15; Martin, op. cit. 319.

[6] Cf. "Hell." III. iv. 15; "Ages." i. 23. Courier brackets this
   sentence [{oti . . . ippeuein}] as a gloss; Martin, p. 323,
   emends.

[7] As to the legal exemption of orphans Schneid. cf. Dem. "Symm."
   182. 15; Lys. "Against Diogeit." 24.

[8] Lit. "metoecs." See "Revenues," ii.

[9] Lit. "men the most antagonistic to the enemy." Is the author
   thinking of Boeotian emigres? Cf. "Hell." VI. iii. 1, 5; Diod. xv.
   46. 6.

[10] Lit. "with the consenting will of the gods these things all may
   come to pass."

And now if the repetition of the phrase throughout this treatise "act with God," surprises any one, he may take my word for it that with the daily or hourly occurrence of perils which must betide him, his wonderment will diminish; as also with the clearer recognition of the fact that in time of war the antagonists are full of designs against each other, but the precise issue of these plots and counterplots is rarely known. To what counsellor, then, can a man apply for advice in his extremity save only to the gods, who know all things and forewarn whomsoever they will by victims or by omens, by voice or vision? Is it not rational to suppose that they will prefer to help in their need, not those who only seek them in time of momentary stress and trouble, but those rather who in the halcyon days of their prosperity make a practice of rendering to Heaven the service of heart and soul?

Printed in the United States
150624LV00003B/10/A